Harambe The Gorilla

Dicks Out For Harambe

Richard Stroker

Copyright © 2012 Richard Stroker

All rights reserved.

Although the author and publisher have made every effort to ensure that the information presented in this book was correct at the present time, the author and publisher do not assume and hereby disclaim any liability to any party for any loss, damage, or disruption caused by errors or omissions, whether such errors or omissions result from negligence, accident, or any other cause.

ISBN-13: 978-1537730752

DISCLAIMER

Names, characters, businesses, places, events, political parties, memes, gorillas and incidents are either the product of the author's imagination or are being used in a fictitious manner. Any resemblance to actual persons, living or dead, or actual events is purely coincidental.

CONTENTS

Disclaimer iii

Tribute 5

Chapter 1 - Fallen Hero 6

Chapter 2 – The Beginning 8

Chapter 3 – Harambe Himself 11

Chapter 4 – Dicks Out For Harambe 14

Chapter 5 – Death 15

ABOUT THE AUTHOR 19

TRIBUTE

This novel is dedicated to the gentle giant Harambe. The world will never again be blessed with such a bright beacon of hope and love. Much like other celebrities and people of importance (such as President John F Kennedy, President Lincoln, John Lennon, Tupac Shakur and Zabuza Momochi), Harambe was murdered before his time. Harambe has transcended reality and will be forever immortalized in our prayers and our hearts. I would like to take this moment to encourage you all to honor our fallen hero. Dicks out old friend, dicks out.

CHAPTER 1 - FALLEN HERO

Like so many other iconic love stories, Romeo and Juliet, Noah and Allie, Haku and Zabuza, this story ends in tragedy.

The rain cascaded down as I held my fallen love in my arms. I could feel his hard, muscular body tense and spasm as his open wound glistened. How could such a small wound be the end of such a gentle and loving giant?

I brushed a hand through the dark tuft of hair on his head and whispered that everything was going to be alright. There was a glint in his beautiful brown eyes that let me know that he appreciated my lie. Harambe raised one of his large hands and delicately caressed my cheek with a hairy knuckle. Suddenly the hand fell from my cheek and the glint in his eye was replaced with a misty hazy blankness.

"Don't leave me!" I screamed while frantically grabbing my fallen lover's hand. "Not now! Not after you have shown me the meaning of love! Not after you made love to me last night. I love you"

There was a loud wailing noise behind me. I turned around and saw a large group of onlookers all distraught at the passing of such an iconic hero. I looked back down at the gorgeous face of my deceased love. The tears from my eyes merged with the rain and sprinkled his still warm lips. I shut my eyes and placed a single caring kiss on his black furry forehead.

My name is Gary Splitter and this is the story of how I fell in love with a handsome gorilla and how our love was prematurely cut short.

CHAPTER 2 – THE BEGINNING

I had been awake, lying in bed, for hours before my alarm finally went off signaling that it was finally 6AM on the 27th of May. Normally I would be excited to start a new job but for some reason I couldn't shake the idea that my life was about to change forever. Maybe it was the fact that my new job role was so alien to me. I was used to working in retail so the shift to zoological based employment was probably the cause of my anxieties.

Suddenly there was a loud cracking noise from outside that sounded distinctly like a gunshot. I instantly rolled out of bed in shock. I moved over to the window and peered outside. It had just been a car back firing.

"Stupid, stupid." I sighed while wiping perspiration from my forehead. "I guess I should get ready for work."

Two hours later I was sat in my car gazing at my new place of employment, Cincinnati Zoo. I had parked by the 'Gorilla World' exhibition. While tapping my fingers along to the radio I glanced in my rear view mirror. There was a distinctive pair of brown eyes staring back at me. I started in surprise and spilled coffee on myself. By the time I glanced back into the mirror the eyes were gone. "You didn't see anything. Stop being stupid," I thought to myself. I waited for the smooth jazz song to finish, and for my nerves to die down, before exiting my car and making my way into the building.

"Ah, you must be Mr. Splitter," came a booming voice the second I crossed the doors threshold. "I am Mr. Mungus, the head of staff, but you can call me Hugh."

Hugh Mungus filled me in with all the duties I would have to perform at the zoo. Most of my duties seemed trivial. I had to clean enclosures, feed the animals, assist customers and restock the gift shop shelves.

"All new employees spend their first day working with Cincinnati's brightest star, Harambe. Today you will be cleaning his enclosure and making sure that he is as happy as can be." Hugh chuckled slightly and began to leave.

"Wait - what's so funny Mr. Mungus?" I inquisitively asked.

Hugh Mungus didn't even glance back at me. "Oh, nothing. Everyone has done this before. Emphasis on D O N E. You will soon find out why they call our zoo SINcinnati!" Came his cryptic reply as he walked away from me.

I stood rooted in place while I pondered his strange reply. I was ashamed by the fact that I was getting a strangely sexual vibe from Mr. Mungus. How very inappropriate for a boss to be hitting on a new employee on their first day. "Oh well." I shrugged, picked up the cleaning gear and made my way to Harambe's enclosure.

CHAPTER 3 – HARAMBE HIMSELF

Once I reached the metal gate to Harambe's enclosure, I took a single steadying breath before entering. I felt incredibly under qualified as I sheepishly made my way into the enclosure. I took a few timid steps into the enclosure and was surprised to find that it was completely empty.

Suddenly there was a loud bang behind me as if a large animal had just dropped to the ground from a small height. I stood stock still in fear. A gentle breeze rhythmically began to caress my neck. It slowly dawned on me that the breeze was actually the breath of Harambe the gorilla!

I began to slow turn my body and was soon face to face with the giant gorilla. I had a sudden flash of recognition as I stared into his brown eyes. I could swear that I had seen those eyes before!

Harambe grunted as he a raised one of his hands and placed it against my cheek. I flinched at the contact. Harambe continued to stare into my eyes as he began stroking my face. An unexplainable surge of electric energy ran throughout my body. His eyes were a perfect shade of brown.

I shook my head lightly. "What am I thinking?" I thought to myself. "That's a crazy thing to think about a gorilla's eyes!" I broke the contact with Harambe and began cleaning his enclosure.

While I worked I could still feel my cheek burning where he had touched me and the hair on the back of my neck was still raised. I glanced back at the gorilla. His eyes were still on me while I worked. There was a hint of fire in his brown eyes – a fire of passion? No one had ever looked at me the way Harambe did in that instance.

About an hour later I had finished cleaning the enclosure. It was time for me to feed Harambe. The sexual tension within the enclosure was almost palpable.

Harambe was sat in one of the corners of his enclosure and had his back to me. I marveled at his muscular form. His back had a silver sheen of hair and I found myself wondering what it would be like to grasp onto that hair during the throws of passionate ecstasy.

I approached the gorilla with a banana in my hand. Before I reached him a smooth jazz song began playing.

"This song! This is the song I was listening to in my car earlier!" I stated in shock.

Harambe turned to face me. His large fingered

hands were clutching a small radio. His top lip curled with desire as he noticed my banana.

I noticed his look. "Oh you want this do you?" I purred as I peeled the skin seductively off the banana. In an instant Harambe crossed the distance between us and placed a firm, but gentle, kiss upon my expectant mouth.

CHAPTER 4 – DICKS OUT FOR HARAMBE

I was shocked. Shocked by what was happening. Shocked that I didn't want it to stop. Shocked that I was enjoying every moment of Harambe's tender touch. I was engaging in gay sex. Gorilla gay sex.

Harambe tender kiss slowly became rougher and rougher. The giant gorilla bared his teeth in a sign of dominance and placed both of his large hairy hands on my buttocks. I melted into his muscular embrace. Harambe's hands explored my buttocks – kneading it, fondling it, squeezing it, spanking it!

Suddenly Harambe tore my zoo keeper overalls off, exposing my expectant body, leaving me in only my underwear. Harambe grunted and pointed towards his lower region. I sank to my knees and stared at his King Kong. The skin on his penis was stretched taut with desire. I ran my tongue along the edge of Harambe's giant banana and he released a primal roar of satisfaction.

After a long period of gorilla falacio, Harambe grasped my arm and pulled me to my feet. He planted a frantic kiss on my neck as his hands roamed to my manhood and began tugging on the hem of my underwear. "Dicks out for Harambe," I purred.

CHAPTER 5 – DEATH

We spent the rest of the day in wild passion and the entire night in each other's loving arms. I had fallen for Harambe: physically fallen to my knees to perform oral sex and metaphorical fallen in love with him.

I woke up with my head on my new love's broad hairy chest. "Good morning you," I giggled. I rolled off his chest and rubbed the sleep from my eyes. "I'm a little sore this morning! Wow. Last night was amazing! Unexpected, but amazing!"

Harambe opened one sleepy eye and curled his top lip in reply. As I began to stand I found his arms wrapped around my waist. "We need to get up! I have work to do!" Before I had a chance to move he had pulled me back onto his chest – my rightful spot!

Suddenly there was a chorus of laughter. I looked up and saw a gaggle of children and parents staring at us. "Fuck!" I screamed! I had completely forgotten that Harambe was a gorilla and that he lived in a zoo. Embarrassment grasped my body and I jumped to my feet. Harambe made a disgruntled noise and beckoned me back to him.

"I'm sorry my love. I just... I can't!" I turned away

from him and placed my head in my hands. "This is all too confusing!" I grabbed my overalls and ran out of the enclosure past a small child.

Five minutes later I was stood in the toilets. I was holding myself in confusion and sadness. How had I let this happen? How could I possibly be in love with a gorilla!?

I mulled over the memories of the previous twenty four hours. Harambe's touch and warmth seemed to engulf my mind. I couldn't stop thinking about his beautiful brown eyes, his gorgeous teasing smile, his muscular arms and his huge King Kong penis. My mind was made up! I loved Harambe and I didn't care who knew it!

I left the toilet and headed back to my love's enclosure. I was fully prepared to confess my love to him and spend the rest of my days in the enclosure with him, wrapped in his tight embrace.

As I pushed open the enclosure door there was a loud BANG. I saw my love, my gorilla, fall to the floor. Harambe's huge arms clutched at his chest and he released a guttural roar. My heart sank. My world went black.

I rushed over to my fallen love. "What happened!?

Are you okay!?"

Harambe stared at me with his loving eyes. I peeled his hands away from his chest and saw a small open wound.

"It can't end like this! Not like this! What a terrible ending to such a beautiful love story!"

ABOUT THE AUTHOR

Richard Stroker started his writing career in the field of academics. Stroker possess a Doctorate degree in Anthropology from Harvard University. Richard also traveled to the United Kingdom to complete a Masters degree in 'Meme Themed Dissing' from the prestigious University of Oxford. Stroker prides himself on his ability to fuse politics, history and homoerotic romance into an unarguably flawless narrative structure, time and time again. Richard Stroker has critically secured his place as being among the best young Harambe-centric homoerotic authors of the 21st century.

Check out our other Harambe Book!

Richard Stroker

Harambe the Gorilla

Printed in Great Britain
by Amazon